Gargoylz

Summer Fun

Gargoylz: grotesque stone creatures found on old buildings, spouting rainwater from the guttering. Sometimes seen causing mischief and mayhem before scampering away over rooftops.

Read all the
Gargoylz adventures!

Summer Fun

Burchett & Vogler

illustrated by Leighton Noyes

GARGOYLZ SUMMER FUN
A RED FOX BOOK 978 1 849 41183 7

First published in Great Britain by Red Fox,
an imprint of Random House Children's Books
A Random House Group Company

This edition published 2010

1 3 5 7 9 10 8 6 4 2

Series created and developed by Amber Caravéo

The Random House Group Limited supports the Forest Stewardship Council
(FSC), the leading international forest certification organization. All our titles
that are printed on Greenpeace-approved FSC-certified paper carry the FSC
logo. Our paper procurement policy can be found at
www.rbooks.co.uk/environment

Mixed Sources
Product group from well-managed
forests and other controlled sources
www.fsc.org Cert no. TT-COC-2139
© 1996 Forest Stewardship Council

Set in Bembo Schoolbook

Red Fox Books are published by Random House Children's Books,
61–63 Uxbridge Road, London W5 5SA

www.**kids**at**randomhouse**.co.uk
www.**rbooks**.co.uk

Addresses for companies within The Random House Group Limited can be
found at: www.randomhouse.co.uk/offices.htm

THE RANDOM HOUSE GROUP Limited Reg. No. 954009

A CIP catalogue record for this book is available from the British Library.

Printed and bound in Great Britain by CPI Bookmarque, Croydon, CR0 4TD

For Ben May - who would have been first in the queue to Splat the Teacher!
- **Burchett & Vogler**

For Rhys Nye who will play for Crystal Palace one day. If he's unlucky.
- **Leighton Noyes**

Hello, I'm the Web Gargoyle.
Look out for me – I'll be hiding in one of the pictures in the book.
When you spot me, be sure to make a note of the secret codeword I'm holding.
The codeword unlocks a secret level of the amazing Gargoylz game on our fabulous website at
www.gargolyz.co.uk

Oldacre Primary School

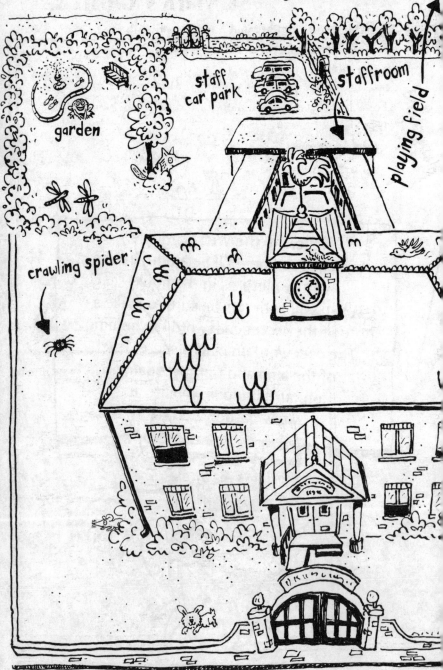

St Mark's Church

Playground

School Report - Max Black

Days absent: 0

Days late: 0

Max is never afraid to make a contribution to history lessons. His demonstration of a battering ram using a broom and a bucket was very realistic, although the resulting hole in the classroom door was not ideal.

I worry that Max only seems to play with Ben Neal, but he assures me he has a lot of friends at the local church.

Class teacher - Miss Deirdre Bleet

Max Black's behaviour this term has been outrageous. He has repeatedly broken school rule number 739: boys must not tell 'knock knock' jokes in assembly. He is still playing pranks with Ben Neal. Mrs Pumpkin is absent again after the exploding paint pot incident. And Mrs Simmer, the head dinner lady, says the mincing machine has never been the same since he fed his maths test into it.

Head teacher - Hagatha Hogsbottom (Mrs)

School Report - Ben Neal

Days absent: 0

Days late: 0

This term Ben has
been very inventive in PE.
However, attempting to tightrope-walk
across the hall was a little dangerous
- and used up all the skipping ropes.
He spends far too much time in class
looking out of the window and waving at
the gravestones in the churchyard. He
would be better learning his spellings - a
word he insists on writing as 'spellingz'.

Class teacher - Miss Deirdre Bleet

Ben Neal is always polite, but I am deeply concerned
about his rucksack. It often looks very full - and
not with school books, I am certain. It has sometimes
been seen to wriggle and squirm. I suspect that he
is keeping a pet in there. If so, it is outrageous and
there will be trouble.

Head teacher - Hagatha Hogsbottom (Mrs)

Contents

1. Competition Crazy

Max Black and Ben Neal roared through the gates of Oldacre Primary School on their imaginary superspy motorbikes. They screeched to a halt, crashed into each other and landed in the compost bin.

"This is very mysterious, Agent Neal," said Max as he picked a banana skin out of his scruffy brown hair. "The playground's empty. It's not Saturday, is it?"

"I wish it was, Agent Black," said Ben, brushing potato peelings off his sweatshirt. "But it's definitely Thursday. We're just

1

late for school."

Suddenly they heard a voice booming away inside the school hall. Max sneaked over to the window and put his spy radar on full power: grey hair, beaky nose, face like a boiled beetroot. He knew what that meant. It was Enemy Agent Mrs Hogsbottom, commonly known as Mrs Hogsbum, codename: Evil Head Teacher.

"We are late," groaned Max. "Mrs Hogsbum's already started assembly."

"We shouldn't have stopped to have that slug race," said Ben. "Time for Secret Plan: Sneak into Assembly."

"We've never had to do that before," said Max with a shudder. "We're usually trying to sneak *out*."

"We might be able to get into the hall behind that curtain," Ben went on, pointing to an open window, "using our superspy slithering powers."

They tiptoed up to the window and peeped over the ledge. The whole school was sitting on the hall floor in neat rows.

"Mrs Hogsbum's droning on more than usual," muttered Max. "Even the teachers look half asleep."

"... and lastly," declared Mrs Hogsbottom, fixing everyone with her beady eyes, "don't forget the school summer fête is on Saturday."

Everyone sat bolt upright and a buzz of chatter went round the hall.

"That's going to be awesome!" whispered Max. "Remember last year?"

Ben nodded eagerly. "Mr Widget slid right off the bouncy castle into the Hook-a-Duck paddling pool."

"I don't know why they blamed us," said Max. "We didn't mean to spill our ice creams on the bouncy castle."

"I want you to bring in any items that your families don't need, for us to sell on our White Elephant stall," Mrs

Hogsbottom was telling the school. "That's the stall where we sell all sorts of things that people don't want any more. So far we have only been given two toast racks and a chipped mug. This is outrageous!"

Max and Ben watched as she raked the school with her laser vision. Those sitting in the front row shrank back in fear.

"Therefore we will be having a competition which you will all enter," she went on. "The pupil who brings in the best item for us to sell will choose which stall they want to run on Saturday."

Max looked at Ben, his eyes shining. "We have to win that prize, Agent Neal!" he gasped.

Ben grinned. "Too right, Agent Black. And there's only one stall we could possibly choose ..."

"Splat the Teacher!" they exclaimed together.

"We'll be able to throw as many wet sponges at them as we like," said Max eagerly. "For free!"

"So we'd better get searching in our houses tonight." Ben nodded over at the church next to the school. "We could ask the gargoylz to come and help."

"Great idea!" whispered Max. "It's always more fun when they're around."

The gargoylz were Max and Ben's secret friends. Only the two boys knew that the stone statues carved all over the church could come to life. No one else ever guessed that they were full of mischief and joined the boys in their tricks and games.

"Shame we haven't got time to chat to them now," said Max, "but we'd better get into assembly before anyone sees us."

At that moment the bell rang and everyone began to file out of the hall. The boys ducked out of sight as their class marched past the window, following Miss Bleet towards the classroom.

"Quick!" whispered Ben. "We'll sneak in at the back of the line."

The boys scrambled onto the window ledge and dropped down behind the curtain. When their last few classmates passed by, they slipped out and followed.

"I think we got away with it," hissed Max as they slid into their seats in the classroom.

"Max Black and Ben Neal!" came Miss Bleet's weedy tones. She peered over her glasses at them. "Where did you spring from? You weren't in assembly."

"Didn't you see us sitting there, miss?" asked Ben.

"It was very exciting," added Max quickly.

"We heard all about the competition for the White Elephant stall. In fact, Ben and I are going to win it. We're going to run Splat the Teacher!"

"You've got no chance," sneered Lucinda Tellingly, tossing her ponytail. "I'm sure to bring in the best donation."

"Poor Lucinda," Ben whispered to Max as the class began chatting about the competition. "She doesn't know about our secret gargoyle helpers."

"No more talk," twittered Miss Bleet, forgetting all about assembly. "Everyone get out your exercise books. I hope you learned your spellings last night because we're going to have a nice test."

Max and Ben looked at each other in horror.

"We didn't have time for spellings," protested Max. "Ben and I had to get to level forty-two on *Killer Gnome Patrol*."

"I'm not listening to any of your excuses," said Miss Bleet. "If you don't know them, you'll have to stay in and help me at playtime."

"It looks like we won't be seeing our gargoyle friends for a while," Max muttered gloomily to Ben.

As they both got nought in their test, Max and Ben spent all playtime mucking out Harry the gerbil's cage. Then they spent all of their lunch break trying to find Harry the gerbil as they'd forgotten to close the cage door.

At last the school day was over.

"Gargoyle time!" declared Max as he and Ben beat everyone else out of school and made a dash for the wall between the playground and the church. As soon

as the playground was
empty, a monkey-faced
creature flew down from
the church spire to land
in front of Max and Ben.

"Greetingz!" he exclaimed in a
growly purr. "We've been looking
for you two all day! We spotted you
climbing into school but you haven't
been out since."

"Hi, Toby," cried Max happily.
"Miss Bleet made us stay in."

A gargoyle with spines
down his back jumped
beside Toby.

"Teacherz spoil everything," he said. "I'd have made a really good bottom burp to stink her out."

"Your special power would have stunk us all out, Barney!" laughed Max.

Every gargoyle had a special power. And they could play super-spectacular tricks with them.

"I'd have burped spiderz at her," said Bart, a little round gargoyle, as he came up to join them. He straightened his gladiator skirt and belched a large red and black spider that scuttled away between the gravestones before fading to nothing.

"We've got some exciting news," Max told them. "We're going in for a competition and the prize is

14

really cool. It's—"

But before he could finish, Toby put his claws to his mouth and gave a deafening whistle. Within a few seconds, two more grinning gargoylz had scrambled onto the wall.

"Hello, Azzan," said Ben. "Hello, Jelly."

"Did you say something about a prize?" asked Jelly eagerly, flapping his pterodactyl wings and nearly sweeping Azzan off the wall.

"Watch it!" cried Azzan, snorting a puff of smoke in surprise. "I almost set fire to your beak!"

Azzan could breathe fire, which was a very useful secret power – most of the time.

"I'll help win the prize . . ." A gargoyle with a fuzzy mane appeared out of thin air right in the middle of everyone, scattering his stony friends.

"You can *all* help, Zack!" laughed Ben.

"The school fête's on Saturday," began Max, "and—"

"Fêtes are super," said Jelly. "I hope there's a treasure hunt."

"And a barbecue," added Azzan.

"Cookiez and cakes! Cookiez and cakes!" chanted Zack.

"I'm sure there will be," Max assured them, "but before that—"

"When the church had a fête, we ate all the jam tarts," Barney informed them. "We got lovely and sticky."

"You should have seen the vicar's face when he found strawberry jam all over the drainpipes!" added Toby.

"Anyway," said Max, wondering if he'd ever manage to tell them the news, "there's this competition. Mrs Hogsbum says that whoever brings

17

in the best thing to sell at the fête gets
to choose a stall to run. We have to win
because we want to run the Splat the
Teacher stall."

The gargoylz scratched their stony
heads.

"Bramblz are really special," said Toby.

"And thistlz," put in Barney. "They're
yummy."

"*You* may love eating them but I don't
think humans do," said Ben. "We have to

go home and find something amazing that everyone will want to buy at the fête."

"And that's where you come in," Max finished. "We're going to search our houses. Toby, Bart and Zack, you come home with me, and Azzan, Jelly and Barney can go and help Ben."

"Good thinking, Agent Black," said Ben. "That way we'll only take half the time to find the most awesome thing in the history of most awesome things."

The gargoylz gave a huge cheer, jumped off the wall and ran off into the long grass of the churchyard.

"Race you," called Zack over his stony shoulder.

"All aboard our superspy motorbikes!" declared Max. "Destination – home!"

Max burst into his bedroom to find Toby and Zack already emptying one of his

drawers. Bart was sitting on the bed, looking grumpy.

"We climbed your ivy," he grumbled, "and I got leaves stuck up my skirt."

"Never mind, Bart," said Max, trying not to laugh. "Help us with our search. You'll soon forget all about it."

Bart humphed and waddled off to inspect Max's bookshelves.

"Now, what will Mrs Hogsbum be really pleased with?" said Max, looking around his room.

"These," declared Zack, waving Max's superhero pyjamas in the air.

"We can't take my pyjamas in," said Max. "They're—"

"How about your pants instead?" shouted Toby, flying around with a pair on his head.

"But I need them," protested Max, stuffing them back in the drawer. "And anyway, clothes aren't special enough to win a competition. Keep looking."

Pop! Zack disappeared.

Max poked his head into a box and started to pull out some dusty old model cars.

Pop! Zack reappeared holding a small pink plastic pony and beaming in delight.

"That's Twinklehooves!" gasped Max. "You've been in my sister's room. How did you survive the flowery smell?"

"I held my nose!" Zack told him, pulling a face.

"You'll have to take it back," said Max. "Jessica's screams would deafen us all if she found it was gone."

Zack disappeared and the pink pony pranced off through the air in his invisible paw.

"How about this?" suggested Toby, trying to pull Max's television off the wall.

"But I love my TV," cried Max. "And how will you watch all your favourite old films if it's gone?"

Toby frowned. "Spluttering gutterz, I hadn't thought of that!" Then his face brightened. "I've got it. You can buy it back at the fête!"

"Great idea," said Max. "But there's just one problem. I don't have enough pocket money."

There was a deep chuckling sound from the corner. Bart had his nose in one of Max's battered old books.

"I've found a great joke," he said. "What do you call a frightened biscuit?"

"I don't know," chorused Toby and Zack. "What *do* you call a frightened biscuit?"

"A cowardy custard cream!" Bart replied,

holding his round
sides as he
rocked with
laughter.
His
friends
rolled
about
on the
floor, chortling.

"That was
funny," said Toby. "I
haven't laughed so much
since Zack put marblz in the vicar's hat
and he thought his brain had come loose."

"I'm glad you've cheered up, Bart," said
Max. "But this isn't helping us find what
we're looking for."

"Yes it is," said Bart happily. "You can
take the joke book in. There's nothing
better than a good joke."

"But the pages are crumpled," Max told

him, "and I've done all the puzzles at the back. I don't think anyone would buy it."

At that moment they heard a loud **ping** from the kitchen and a delicious smell wafted up into the room.

The gargoylz sniffed the air eagerly, their tongues hanging out.

"What's that?" asked Bart, dropping the joke book. "It smellz wonderful."

"Time for treats," declared Zack,

bouncing up and down.

"That was the bread maker," said Max. "It's just finished making a loaf." His eyes lit up. "That's given me an awesome idea!" he exclaimed. "I'll take the bread maker into school. It's sure to win the prize. Everyone loves fresh bread!"

"And your mum can buy it back at the fête!" said Toby brightly.

Max crept out of the door. The next moment he was back, carrying a big white machine with a dangling cord.

27

He opened the lid, using his pyjama top
as an oven glove, and lifted out a loaf of
fresh, warm bread.

"I'll give you a bit off the crust, then
I'll take it back to the kitchen," he told his
gargoyle friends.

Zack grabbed the loaf, jumped up onto
the bed and took a huge bite out of the
middle. Toby and Bart joined in, and soon
all that was left was a pile of crumbs.

Max's bedroom door was suddenly
flung open. Zack vanished and Toby and

Bart dived under the duvet as Mrs Black appeared.

"Have you seen the . . . ?" She trailed off as she spotted the empty bread maker. Then she strode over and picked it up. "You've eaten the whole loaf!" she exclaimed crossly, pointing at the pile of crumbs.

"I can explain," burbled Max.

An enormous gargoyle burp burst out from under the duvet.

"Really, Max!" exclaimed his mum.

Max put his hand over his mouth. "Pardon me," he said quickly. "Sorry I ate the bread. I was really hungry."

But his mother wasn't listening. She'd caught sight of a line of big black spiders marching across Max's pillow. She gave a scream and dashed out of the room.

"Good plan, Bart!" exclaimed Max, pulling back the duvet. "Mum was so scared she forgot to tell me off."

"It was an accidental burp," admitted Bart, rubbing his tummy. "I've eaten too much."

Pop! Zack reappeared. "Lucky escape, but now you've got nothing to take!" he said, shaking his lion's mane.

"It'll be all right," said Max. "Ben's sure to find something for the fête. You lot had better get yourselves home to the church."

Der-ring! went Max's doorbell the next morning.

Max took the stairs two at a time and flung the door open eagerly to find his best friend on the doorstep.

"What have you found?" he exclaimed. Ben held out his empty hands and shrugged.

"Our dream of running the Splat the Teacher stall is doomed," Max groaned.

"The gargoylz had plenty of ideas," said Ben. "The lawnmower, my computer, a cupboard full of cookies. Then Azzan found one

really cool thing – my dad's football
signed by the Oldacre Rovers team."

"That would win, no problem,"
declared Max, cheering up. "Where is it?"

"I couldn't bring it," said Ben with a
sigh. "When Dad saw me carrying it out
of the house this morning, he snatched it
off me. I tried to get it back but he started
to cry so I had to let him keep it."

"Bad luck," said Max. "It was a good
idea though. We'd better get to school."

He set off gloomily down the path.

"Wait for me," called Ben. "I'm going to need some help carrying these."

Max turned to find his friend staggering under the weight of a huge bag of golf clubs.

"Tricked you!" said Ben with a grin. "I hid them in the hedge."

"Where did you get them?" asked Max in amazement.

"After Jelly, Barney and Azzan had gone home, I told Dad about the competition and he said I could have them. The only time he used them he whacked himself on the nose and a squirrel ran off with the ball."

"We're sure to win the competition now," said Max happily. "Mrs Hogsbottom's the judge, and your dad's clubs are just the sort of thing old people like her will want to buy. We must show the gargoylz."

"Great idea. Let's go," Ben cried, punching the air. "Splat the Teacher, here we come!"

2. Where's the Elephant?

Max and Ben staggered along to school, dragging the heavy golf bag behind them.

"I can't wait to run the Splat the Teacher stall tomorrow!" declared Ben.

"It'll be awesome," agreed Max.

They lugged the precious clubs across the playground and into the school hall. Mrs Hogsbottom was standing guard over a pile of peculiar objects on the stage, while everyone milled around waiting for her to announce the winner of the competition.

Max and Ben hoicked up the golf bag

and stuck it right
in the middle.

"Humph!"
grunted Mrs
Hogsbottom as
she wrote their
names on a
sticky label and
slapped it on
the bag.

"Let's check
out what the others have brought in,"
said Ben.

There was an assortment of old books,
frilly lampshades and plastic flowers.

"Nothing's as good as our golf
clubs," Max told him. He peered at a
small envelope labelled LUCINDA
TELLINGLY. "Lucinda hasn't even tried.
Who's going to want to buy one silly
envelope?"

Mrs Hogsbottom inspected all the

items closely, scribbling comments on a clipboard. Then she turned to the waiting pupils.

"You've all done very well," she admitted. She checked her clipboard. "Even Max Black and Ben Neal have brought in something very good for the White Elephant stall."

Max and Ben did a secret low-five. "We'll make the sponges extra drippy," whispered Max.

"And use really cold water," hissed Ben.

"But" – Mrs Hogsbottom hadn't finished – "the winner is . . . Lucinda Tellingly."

"It can't be," Max burst out. "She just brought in a scrappy old envelope!"

Lucinda whipped round, a smug smile on her face. "An envelope containing two VIP tickets to see *Tap Dancing on Ice* being filmed," she boasted. "My mum works on the programme. *Everyone* will want to buy the tickets."

"Well done, Lucinda," barked Mrs Hogsbottom. "It's so good we'll put it in the raffle. Now, which stall would you like to run?"

"Please may I run . . ." began Lucinda.

Max and Ben crossed their fingers behind their backs.

"Not Splat the Teacher," muttered Ben.

"The Splat the Teacher stall!" announced Lucinda with an evil smirk at the boys.

"Disaster!" groaned Max.

"Excellent!" said Mrs Hogsbottom. "Now we'll pick the rest of the stallholders." She picked up a box full of folded pieces of paper. "As Ben Neal and

Max Black's item was so good, they can go first," she announced.

Ben plunged his hand among the papers and had a good rummage around. He pulled one out and unfolded it. His face fell. "Sorry, Max," he said. "We've got the White Elephant stall." He pointed to the things piled up on the stage. "We're going to have to sell all this junk."

At break time Max and Ben went to look for the gargoylz.

"Greetingz!" called a voice, and Toby, Barney and Jelly scrambled up onto the wall in an excited rush.

"Did you win?" asked Barney, his round doggy eyes bright with excitement.

"No," said Max. "We've got to run the White Elephant stall."

"Dangling drainpipes!" said Barney. "That sounds like a lovely stall."

"Leave it with us," added Toby. "We'll make sure it's the best stall in the whole fête."

Bringggg! The bell went.

"See you at lunch time," called Jelly cheerily.

Max and Ben trudged back into school.

"At least *they're* pleased about our stall," said Ben. "Perhaps it's not going to be so bad after all."

"I wonder what the gargoylz have got planned," said Max as they made their way back outside later to see their little stony friends. "It's a boring stall. I can't think of anything."

"They look as if they're bursting with ideas!" laughed Ben when they peered over the wall.

A line of grinning gargoylz sat under a stone angel. They jumped to their feet when they saw the boys and dashed over.

"We've got everything ready for the elephants," Toby burst out.

"They're going to sleep up on the roof with us until the fête," said Azzan.

Jelly nodded his pterodactyl beak enthusiastically. "It'll be terribly jolly."

"Well, it will be once we've worked out how to get them up there," added Bart solemnly. "We were thinking of making a special catapult."

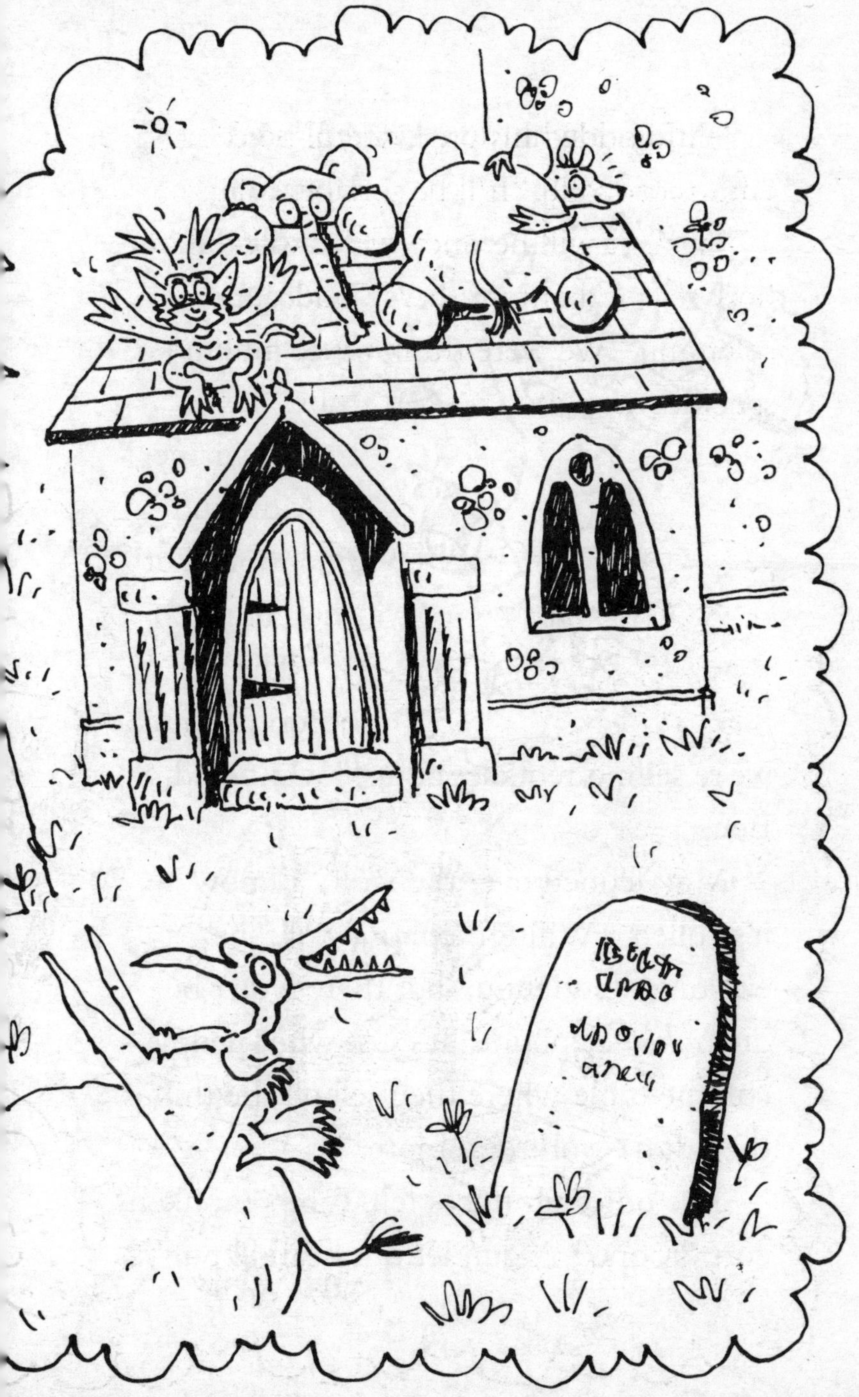

"And see what I've knitted," said

Barney proudly. He held out a long blue tube. "It's a trunk-warmer."

Max and Ben looked at each other.

"The gargoylz think we're selling real elephants!" whispered Ben.

Max leaned over the wall. "I know it's called a White Elephant stall," he explained patiently, "but there won't be any *actual* elephants. It's just what people call the table where they sell all the things they don't want any more."

The gargoylz' faces fell. Toby's monkey ears drooped, Azzan let out a small puff of smoke and Jelly began to melt in disappointment.

"Won't there be even *one* elephant?" asked Barney, waving his trunk-warmer.

"I wouldn't count on it," said Max.

"I was looking forward to seeing the elephants," sighed Jelly. "It would have been super."

The other gargoylz nodded sadly.

Max and Ben were so busy trying to cheer up the gargoylz that they were nearly late for afternoon school. They rushed into their classroom. Someone was standing at the front. Max turned on his spy radar: long wavy hair, rope sandals, paint on the end of her nose. He knew what that meant. It was Enemy Agent Miss Pastel, codename: Paint-splattered Art Teacher. She sometimes came in to teach art to Year Four.

"We've got lots of work to do this afternoon," she told the class brightly. "You're all going to be making signs and decorations for the fête."

There was a happy murmur of chatter at this. Miss Pastel put up her hand for quiet. "And just to make it even more fun," she went on, "whoever does the best work gets a free go on the stall of their choice tomorrow. You can start now and finish at home if you want to."

Max's eyes lit up. "That means we could still get a free go on Splat the Teacher," he whispered.

"And I've had a brilliant idea!" Ben whispered back. "We should make a really eye-catching sign for our stall – an enormous elephant."

They put a huge piece of card on the floor and began to draw.

"It doesn't look much like an elephant," said Ben critically. "More like a balloon on a stick."

"It'll be all right when we get the ears on," Max assured him.

By the end of
the afternoon,
Max and Ben's
giant elephant
was looking
very cheerful.
It had one
floppy tusk, a
toothy smile
and the words
WHITE ELEPHANT STALL
– EVERYTHING YOU NEED scrawled
on its round tummy.

"It's awesome," sighed Ben happily.
"We're sure to win with this."

Max checked around to see what the
rest of the class had done. "I'm not so sure,"
he said. "Lucinda's painted her 'Splat the
Teacher!' to look as if it's really dripping."

"And Duncan's Lucky Dip sign
makes me want to have a go right now!"
groaned Ben.

"Don't despair, Agent Black," said Ben. "We haven't finished. We've still got to make the decorations for our stall. We'll just have to make sure they're super-duper awesomely brilliant."

"I know how we can cheer the gargoylz up too," said Max. "They love drawing and stuff. Let's get them to help."

"Great plan," exclaimed Ben. "Let's all meet at my house this afternoon."

The bell rang for the end of school.

"Good work, everyone," called Miss Pastel. "I'll see you in the playground tomorrow at eleven o'clock sharp. That'll give you an hour to arrange your decorations before the fête starts."

The pupils made for the door but found their way blocked by a

solid figure. Max's spy radar went into overdrive: shaved head, big fists, snarling grin. He knew what that meant. It was Enemy Agent Barry Price, also known as The Basher, codename: School Bully.

"Before anyone leaves," said Barry, waving a piece of paper menacingly at them, "you've got to sign my list promising to make some cakes for my stall. Or else."

Everyone did, even Miss Pastel.

The boys
jumped into
their imaginary
superspy
racing car,
whizzed into
the churchyard
and told the
gargoylz to
meet them at

Ben's house as soon as possible.

After some extra-nifty racing-car
moves they were soon in Ben's kitchen
getting supplies for their work.

"We've got to make decorations for the
fête," Max told Mrs Neal, "and we need
some bright sparkly stuff."

"We could use this!" cried Ben,
grabbing a big tube of glitter and a pile of
card from the kitchen table.

"I'm using that," said his mother.
"I'm making birthday cards. But I've got

something much better for you. There's lots of shiny material and sequins left over from when your dad joined that ballroom dancing class. You can use it to make the kind of bunting you often see at fêtes and fairs." She pulled a huge box out from under the stairs.

"See this nice red satin?" she said, smoothing the fabric out on the kitchen table. "All you need to do is cut it carefully into diamond shapes, fold them in half over a long piece of string, and then stick on the sequins."

"Awesome," said Max. "It'll look just like the stalls at a proper fairground. Thanks, Mrs Neal."

They picked up the
box and made for the
stairs.

"By the way, Mum,"
Ben called over his
shoulder, "I've signed you
up to make fifty cupcakes
for the fête tomorrow."

Leaving Ben's mother
gulping for air, the boys
darted up the stairs and
into Ben's bedroom.

There was a scuffling
noise and three stony tails
disappeared in a flash.

"It's only us," said Max.
"You don't have to hide."

"We've been waiting
here for hourz!" Jelly complained, climbing
down from the curtains.

"Dayz," put in Toby, popping up from a
pile of Ben's clothes on the floor.

"Weeks," said Barney.

"What have you got there?" asked Jelly. "Looks like jolly good fun."

Ben told them how to make the bunting.

"Dangling drainpipes, let's get stuck in," said Toby. He grabbed the glue and splattered it all over the shiny fabric in huge blobs. Barney and Jelly took pawfuls of sequins and tossed them into the air.

"Hold on!" said Ben, horrified. "You're making my bedroom all girly. The sequins are supposed to go on the material."

"Some of
them have,"
said Toby
helpfully. "Shall
I start cutting?"
He took a pair
of scissors and
picked up a shiny piece
of red material from the mess on the floor.

"No!" cried Ben, snatching the scissors
away from him. "That's my favourite
football shirt!"

After the boys had got the gargoylz
organized, they all set to work cutting and
gluing the sparkling diamond shapes onto
the string.

"Awesome!" said Max, sitting back
on his heels at last. "We've got enough
bunting here to decorate the whole of
Oldacre."

The floor was covered in bright
garlands of gleaming triangles and the

gargoylz were covered in sequins. Three
jumpers and a woolly hat now had
diamond-shaped holes.

The bedroom door flew open with a
crash. Mrs Neal stood there holding a tray
of juice and cookies.

"Freeze!" Toby hissed to his friends.

"Good gracious!" gasped Ben's mum.
"You've worked really hard. You certainly
deserve your snack." She put down
the tray.

"Though I'm not sure about those statues," she added, peering at the frozen gargoylz. "Where do they fit in with the decorations?"

"They're . . . erm . . ." began Ben.

". . . garden ornaments for our stall!" finished Max quickly.

"They're a bit ugly," said Ben's mum as she left.

"Phew!" said Ben. "That was close."

"Ugly?" exclaimed Jelly.

"She didn't mean it," Ben assured him.

"Garden ornaments?" huffed Toby.

"We had to say something to keep your secret," said Max.

"I suppose that's all right then." Toby gave a huge grin. "Time to go back to the church, gargoylz."

Jelly began to gather up the

bunting. "Hold onto the end for us, Max," he said. "We'll hang it out of the window and swing down on it."

"And then we'll take it to school for you," added Barney. "By the time you arrive tomorrow we'll have decorated the whole stall."

The gargoylz scrambled onto the windowsill.

"I can't wait for the fête," said Toby as he swung down the bunting after his friends. "It'll be even more fun than when we used the vicar's braces to bungee-jump off the steeple!"

The gargoylz scuttled off into the bushes, paws full of the bright triangles and string.

"This is going to be a fête to remember," declared Max happily as he and Ben waved their friends off.

3. Splat the Teacher!

It was Saturday, the day of the Oldacre
School Summer Fête. Max and Ben shot
into the playground in their imaginary
superspy jet boots. The place had been
transformed. Decorated stalls and games
filled every nook and cranny. There was
a coconut shy, a lucky dip, a sweet stall
and, right in the middle, Splat the Teacher.
Lucinda was standing next to it, gawping
in disbelief at something sparkling brightly
by the staffroom window. The boys
followed her gaze.

"It's our stall!" gasped Max. "The

gargoylz have done an amazing job decorating it. They've even found our elephant sign."

The boxes of goods, the table and its stripy roof were completely covered in sparkly red flags. The rest of the bunting ran up a drainpipe, three times round the clock tower and was tied in a messy knot on the weathervane.

The other stallholders were hurriedly finishing their displays as Miss Pastel walked round to judge the best decorations. She stopped in delight at the White Elephant table.

"Well done, boys!" she exclaimed. "Your decorations are marvellous." Then her eyes followed the trail of bunting and she looked anxious. "You didn't climb on the roof to put those up, did you?" she asked.

Max shook his head. "Oh no, miss," he said with a wink at Ben. "The wind probably carried the flags up there."

"Or a passing pigeon," suggested Ben.

"Well, I'm pleased to say that Max Black and Ben Neal have won the prize for the best decorations," Miss Pastel announced loudly, handing the boys a paper token each.

"Cool!" yelled Max. "We'll get a free go on Splat the Teacher!"

"We must thank the gargoylz,"  whispered Ben. "We've just got time to see them before we set everything out on our stall."

The boys sidled over to the wall to peer at the church roof.

"There's no sign of them," said Max. "I wonder where they've gone. They won't want to miss the fête."

"Outrageous!" bellowed a voice. Max's spy radar came to life: grey hair, beaky

nose, jabbing finger. He knew what
that meant. It was Enemy Agent Mrs
Hogsbottom, commonly known as Mrs
Hogsbum, codename: Evil Head Teacher.

"School rule number seven
hundred and eighty-one," shouted Mrs
Hogsbottom. "Boys on the White Elephant
stall must have their items ready when the
head teacher wants to price them with her
special head teacher price-labelling gun."

Max and Ben sped back to their stall
and quickly set out the things for sale. Mrs
Hogsbottom planted herself in front of
the table. Max put out
a chipped teapot;
Mrs Hogsbottom
aimed her gun
at it and a
£1.50 label
appeared on
its side. Ben
plonked down a

box of assorted dolls, the gun clicked and the next minute they all had 99p stickers on their noses.

"Don't stand still, Agent Black," hissed Ben, "or she'll put a sticker on you too!"

At last the table was heaving with things for sale – tea towels, toast racks and tin trays all had prices stuck firmly on them. Mrs Hogsbottom strode off to the cake stall, price gun at the ready.

Ben pulled out his dad's golf clubs. "We nearly forgot these," he told Max. "Now they've missed getting a label. We can charge what we want."

There was a growly purr from the bag and a pair of stony ears popped up, followed by Toby's monkey face.

"Greetingz!" he said with a grin. "This is a nice bag but you

70

should get rid of these sticks." He pointed
at the golf clubs. "They're taking up all
the room."

"We were wondering where you
gargoylz had got to," said Max in delight.

"Look out!" warned Ben suddenly.
"Mrs Hogsbum's seen the golf bag. She's
coming back."

Horrified, Toby disappeared into the
bag just as the head teacher aimed the
gun at it with a loud **click**. There was
a gasp from inside. When she'd gone, he

71

peeped out again.

"I've been shot!" he said weakly.

"It wasn't a real gun," Ben explained.

Suddenly there was an ear-splitting screech from across the playground.

"There's a rat in the raffle!" yelled a girl from Year Six.

Max and Ben looked over at the big drum that was full of raffle tickets. A stony tail was disappearing inside.

Toby beamed. "That'll be Azzan," he said. "He's playing hide-and-seek with Jelly. The other gargoylz are around here somewhere too."

"We're in for some fun then!" exclaimed Max.

"Welcome, everybody." The head teacher's voice suddenly boomed out through her loudhailer. The ornaments on the White Elephant stall rattled, and at the coconut shy several coconuts fell off their stands. *"I now declare the Oldacre Primary School Fête open! I order you to have fun."*

The crowds obediently swarmed around the playground, making for their favourite stalls and games.

One of the dads came up to Max and Ben. "I've got a donation for your stall," he said, adding doubtfully, "I don't know if anyone will buy it though." He produced a small china object and held it out.

"A white elephant!" cried Max, taking it from him. "Thanks. That's perfect."

When he'd gone, the boys looked at each other.

"Barney's going to love this," said Ben.

"Let's buy it for him straight away," suggested Max.

All of a sudden the boys heard a loud clicking sound. The next moment Mrs Hogsbottom's gun had swooped on the elephant and stuck a label on its trunk.

"Three pounds!" gasped Max in dismay as the head teacher prowled off towards the cake stall. The boys quickly checked the coins in their pockets. "We can't afford that."

"A fantastic idea has just popped into my superspy brain, Agent Black," said Ben. "We can ask our mums for extra cash when they get here."

"Simple but brilliant, Agent Neal," said Max, positioning the elephant at the back of the table.

Soon they'd sold two battered picture frames, a three-legged stool with one leg missing, and a tea cosy to an old man who thought it was a hat.

Then disaster struck. A little girl trotted up, pointed to the white elephant and held out her money.

"I'll have that please," she lisped.

Max and Ben looked at her in horror.

"It's not for sale," Max told her.

"Yes it is," she insisted. "It's got a price tag on it."

"Wouldn't you like something else instead?" asked Ben desperately.

"I only like elephants," said the little girl. "Elephants and fairies."

"How about this?" Max held out a china plate with a ballerina on it.

"Boys are so silly," the girl said pityingly. "That's not a fairy. She hasn't got wings."

"Yes she has," Max told her. "She's taken them off while she's dancing. And it's only one pound fifty."

The little girl considered this. Max and Ben held their breath.

"All right," she said at last. "I'll have the plate."

"That was a dodgy moment!" gasped Max when she'd gone. "I'll hide the elephant behind this vase. With any luck no one will notice it."

"What's all this rubbish?" The boys turned to see Barry Price striding up to them. He had an iced bun in one hand and a chocolate muffin in the other. "Bet you wish you were on the cake stall like me," he sneered, ramming the bun into his mouth in one go, "instead of having this load of junk to sell."

Chuckling evilly, he barged into the corner of the stall and ran off. The china elephant shook and wobbled and toppled off the table. Max threw himself forward and caught it just before it smashed on the ground.

"Awesome goalkeeping skills," gasped Ben.

"I wish we'd got enough money to buy this now," said Max as he got to his feet, clutching the elephant. "Then we could sneak it off to Barney. Funny – we haven't seen any gargoylz around for a while."

Ben grinned and pointed at the Hoopla stall, where children were throwing rings at an assortment of prizes laid out on the playground. A little boy was throwing his hoop at a toy car. Max and Ben could see he was going to miss, but at the last minute the car suddenly slid across the ground and the hoop landed right over the top of it.

"Good old Zack!" laughed Max, catching sight of a stone ear. Zack's secret power was amazing, but he didn't always remember to stay completely invisible when he got excited.

The little boy ran off in delight with his car, leaving the girl in charge of the stall scratching her head, puzzled.

Ben looked at the wooden Splat the Teacher board with a picture of a donkey on it. It had a hole where the head should be, and Miss Bleet's anxious face was poking through it.

"I don't know why she's looking so worried," said Max. "Lucinda's making sure the Splat the Teacher sponges are practically dry before she lets anyone throw them."

"And she's giving the victims a towel afterwards," groaned Ben. "She's such a creep."

Max grinned. "Just wait till it's our turn." He glanced over at the crowd of people streaming in through the school gate. "But I think we're going to be too busy for a while."

"My mum's here at last!" exclaimed Ben as a frazzled Mrs Neal staggered across the playground carrying an enormous cake tin. "Now we can get some money to buy the elephant." He waved. "Over here, Mum!"

"Can't stop for long!" panted Mrs Neal. "I've got to take these to the cake stall." She opened the lid and the boys forgot all about the money they needed as they gazed longingly at the cakes inside.

"They look wonderful!" gasped Max. "How did you do the coloured icing?"

"I used food colouring," Ben's mum told him. "It's taken me all morning. Now I must deliver them safely." She shut the lid quickly and scuttled off before Max and Ben could dive in.

"Your mum's given me a super-cool idea," said Max mysteriously. "I won't be a second."

Before Ben could reply, he had shot off towards the school kitchen. Ben had just sold a dusty fruit bowl and a set of hankies with pixies on them when Max reappeared clutching a small green bottle.

"Green food colouring, Agent Neal," he told Ben, his eyes sparkling with mischief. "I had to wait until Mrs Simmer was busy with the tea urn, then I crawled in and grabbed it. We'll sneak over and pour it into Lucinda's bucket. That should make Splat the Teacher much more interesting!"

"First-class idea, Agent Black!" declared
Ben. "Our superspy brains are working on
turbo today."

There was a
sudden **POP!**
and a clatter,
and Zack
appeared in one
of the saucepans
on the stall.

"You did a
good job with the
Hoopla, Zack," Max told him.

"Too good," said Zack with a grin.
"Mrs Hogsbum had to close it down
because they ran out of prizes."

"Here she comes now," warned Max.
"You'd better disappear."

But it was too late. Mrs Hogsbottom
was bearing down on them. Zack froze in
the saucepan, a ghastly gargoyle grin on
his face.

The head teacher cast her beady eyes over the stall. Then she saw Zack in the pan. "Outrageous!" she boomed. "This one hasn't got a price." She whipped the gun out of her pocket and clicked a label onto  Zack's forehead. "It's so ugly I don't think it will sell," she told the boys, "but we might get rid of it for five pence." And with that she swept off.

"I've been shot!" moaned Zack. "I've been shot." He fell over backwards in the saucepan with his feet in the air.

Toby scurried down the bunting and landed on the handle. "It's OK," he said. "It's not a real gun."

Zack scrambled to his feet in relief.

"Shame the head teacher thinks you're ugly and only worth five p," laughed Toby.

"Do you want to get your own back

on Mrs Hogsbum for being so rude?"
Max said quickly before they could start
arguing.

Zack nodded eagerly.

Max put the bottle of food colouring
into his paws. "She's just about to take her
turn on Splat the Teacher. If you put all
of this into the bucket of water, we'll see
what she looks like with a green face."

POP! Zack was gone. Nobody noticed
the little bottle floating through the air

on its own. Soon the water in Lucinda's
bucket was bright green.

Mrs Hogsbottom stuck her head

through the hole in the board. The
wooden donkey looked scary with her
scowling face staring out of it.

"Roll up! Roll up!" she bellowed.

The fair-goers looked at each other
in horror. No one dared have a go – not
even the parents.

"I'm itching to grab a sponge," sighed
Max. "But we can't leave our stall.
Someone might buy the elephant if we're
not here to protect it."

Mrs Hogsbottom was looking even
more cross than normal. "Outrageous!"
she boomed. "School rule number one
thousand and seven – Students must throw
sponges at the
head teacher
when she's
taking her turn
on Splat the
Teacher." She
twisted round

and spotted Lucinda. "Come on, girl!" she
barked. "Splat me!"

Lucinda gave a little whimper of fear
and picked up a sponge. She was shaking
so much that she dropped it in the bucket
without noticing the colour of the water.

"Hurry up!" shouted Mrs Hogsbottom.

Lucinda closed her eyes, drew out the
dripping sponge, and lobbed it at the
donkey.

SPLAT! The head teacher's face turned

bright green.

Suddenly all the children were clamouring to throw a sponge at Mrs Hogsbottom.

"Her face is turning as green as a cabbage," said Ben, a huge grin on his face.

As they watched, there was a **click!** and Miss Bleet stepped forward and took a picture of their stall.

"Lovely," she said in her quavery voice. "I'm taking photos for the school newsletter and I think your decorations are—"

She broke off as a familiar voice roared across the playground.

"Take my picture!"

Miss Bleet turned to look at the Splat the Teacher stall. A green-faced Mrs Hogsbottom was beckoning to her.

"Er . . . are you sure?" Miss Bleet quavered.

"Of course I'm sure," bellowed the head teacher.

Shaking from head to toe, Miss Bleet took the photo and turned to run. But Mrs Hogsbottom, looking like an angry Brussels sprout, left her cardboard donkey and swooped down on her.

"Show me the picture," she demanded. Miss Bleet obeyed. The head teacher stared at the photograph of her scowling green face for a moment. Then, "OUTRAGEOUS!" she shrieked. "School rule number one thousand and eight. Students must not turn the head teacher green when she's taking her turn on Splat the Teacher!" And she stormed off to her office.

"That was a spectacular trick, Agent Neal," gasped Max when they'd managed to stop laughing.

"Splashtastic, Agent Black," agreed Ben. Then he looked worried. "I forgot to ask my mum for some money," he cried. "We need to buy the elephant before someone else does."

There was no sign of Ben's mother, but Mrs Hogsbottom, her face now red from scrubbing, was bearing down on them with a piece of paper and a marker pen in her hand. The boys gulped. What evil plan did she have in mind now?

"The fête will be finishing in half an

hour," she said, "so I'm putting the prices down."

She wrote EVERYTHING MUST GO – ALL ITEMS ONLY 10P in big bold letters on the paper and stuck it firmly on the stall.

When she'd gone, the boys stared at each other. They could hardly believe their luck.

"You know what this means?" Ben whispered. "We can afford to buy the elephant for Barney now!"

Max hurriedly got out a ten-p piece and put it in the pot. "Barney's going to be so pleased," he said, carefully placing the elephant in an empty box under the stall.

"Awesome!" said Ben. "We've turned Mrs Hogsbum green *and* got a great present for Barney. This is the best fête in the history of best fêtes!"

4. The Lucky Nip Stall

The playground was full of happy fête-goers. Max and Ben were so busy on the White Elephant stall that soon their table was beginning to look a bit empty.

Miss Pastel came up. "You haven't had the free goes you won, boys," she told them. "I'll take over here while you use your tokens."

"Thanks, miss!" yelled the boys.

"Splat the Teacher, here we come!" declared Max as they zoomed past the Treasure Hunt table and skidded round the barbecue.

"Shame Mrs Hogsbum won't be our target," said Ben. "I'd get my sponge and— Oof!" Someone rushed past, knocking him flying into a pile of footballs at the Beat the Goalie stall.

"Who did that?" he gasped, bouncing back to his feet.

"It was Barry," Max told him. "And he's up to no good as usual."

The Basher cannoned into the Raffle drum, knocking it off the stand and spilling all the tickets. Then he rampaged

on to the
Welly
Wanging
game,
grabbed a handful
of boots and flung them
into the hedge. "I
win!" he growled. "I
threw the wellies the
furthest."

Suddenly he spotted
the Whack-a-Rat stall,
manned by the boys' classmate, Gavin.
A small boy was holding the whacking
bat and waiting to hit the toy rat when it
dropped out of the tube.

"Watch out, Gavin!" yelled Max
desperately.

But it was too late. The Basher
snatched the bat and swung it hard,
missing the rat completely and knocking
the tube off its stand. The tube sailed

up into the air and landed on
Gavin's head.

"Got the rat!" announced
Barry nastily.

"Mrs Hogsbum's over
by the coconut shy,"
said Ben. "She'll see
him and sort him out."
But Barry snatched
up a prize from the
Whack-a-Rat and
ran back to his own stall.
When Mrs Hogsbottom
went past, he was serving an
old lady with a cup of tea and a dainty
cake and smiling an innocent smile.

Max looked back at the trail of
destruction that Barry had left. "We'd
better have our free go before he wrecks
the whole fête," he said. "We'll use
superspy sprinting speed and go to Splat
the Teacher straight away."

Mr Widget, the science teacher, had his head in the hole now. He peered out over his glasses, looking nervous when he saw Max and Ben approaching.

Max handed his token to Lucinda, who scowled and handed him a well-squeezed sponge in return.

"No thanks," said Max firmly. "I'll choose my own." Before Lucinda could protest he'd picked up the biggest, most

absorbent sponge he could find. "I'm going to get this really wet and give Mr Widget a good soaking," he announced.

He dunked the sponge deep into the water and was about to lob it at the science teacher when Barry charged through the stall, sending the sponges flying. He barged into Lucinda, who fell backwards with a yell and landed – **splash!** – right in the bucket.

She struggled to get up but
immediately toppled over, the bright
orange bucket stuck firmly to her
bottom. She crawled about, dripping and
shrieking.

"She looks like a demented tortoise!"
whispered Max, trying not to laugh.

Ben stuffed his fist in his mouth but the
snorts were escaping. The boys gave up
and laughed until their tummies hurt.

Mr Widget rushed over and tried to pull the bucket off, but Lucinda was stuck fast. Lucinda's friends, Tiffany and Poppy, joined in to make a chain with Miss Bleet on the end.

"Now it's a Tug of War," burst out Ben. The boys laughed even harder.

"Shame you've lost your free go," said Ben as the bucket finally came free of Lucinda, and Mr Widget, Tiffany, Poppy and Miss Bleet fell backwards in a heap on the grass. "Lucinda's got your token."

"I don't mind," said Max cheerfully. "The Soaking of Lucinda Tellingly was much more fun than lobbing a sponge at old Widget."

"You're right," said Ben. He looked around the fête. "What's the next best stall . . . Lucky Dip!"

They charged over to the big wooden tub where Duncan from their class was taking the money. It was filled with sawdust but the boys knew that deep inside were wrapped prizes, just waiting to be picked out.

Ben handed over his token and rolled up his sleeve. "Here I go," he said.

A shadow fell over the tub. It was The Basher.

"I'm going first!" he shouted, elbowing Ben to one side.

"It's *my* go," protested Ben. "Isn't it, Duncan?"

"Well . . ." Duncan looked terrified. "As Barry's already started, he might as well finish," he mumbled lamely.

"But he hasn't paid," said Max.

Barry glowered at him.

"I'm sure he will in a minute," stammered poor Duncan.

The Basher thrust his hand into the sawdust and rummaged around. "I'm going to give every present a good feel," he said, smirking. "That way I can pick the best one."

"That's not fair!" exclaimed Max. He gulped as Barry frowned at him. It was scary standing up to The Basher, but someone had to.

"I'll show you what's fair," muttered Barry, swishing the sawdust around. "I'm going to take them all— OW!"

He gave a high-pitched shriek, whipped his hand out and held up his thumb. He stared at it, his mouth hanging open.

"What's the matter?" asked Duncan nervously.

"Something bit me!" gasped Barry. "And it really hurt! Mum!" he wailed, running off into the crowd. "Mum! Something bit me!"

"I can guess what caused that little scene, Agent Neal," whispered Max.

"A gargoyle," Ben whispered back. "I'm going to find out which one." He turned to Duncan. "I'll have my go now," he told him.

He pushed his hand through the rough sawdust and felt around. There were lots of packages, all wrapped in paper. "Nothing

gargoyle-shaped," he muttered to Max. "Or stony." He thrust his hand down to the very bottom of the barrel and his fingers closed on a squishy ball.

Suddenly it wriggled.

"Jelly!" he gasped. Duncan stared at him. "I mean, I've found a ball that feels like jelly," he added quickly. "That's what I want."

Ben pulled out a rubbery purple ball covered in sawdust and showed it to Max.

"Awesome!" said Max. "Let's . . . play with it back at our stall."

They ran back and Ben put the ball

under the
White
Elephant
table.
When Miss
Pastel had
gone, it
twitched and
melted into
a gooey purple
puddle. Then it gurgled
and bubbled and turned into their little
pterodactyl friend.

"Hello there, chaps!" said Jelly as he
shook the sawdust off his wings. "Thanks
for rescuing me. I was hiding from Azzan
when that awful Basher boy started
prodding me, so I nipped him with my
beak."

"It was a great trick," said Max.

"I couldn't leave you in there," Ben
explained, "even though it meant I didn't

get a prize. In fact neither of our free goes have gone according to plan."

"But you did get a prize," said Jelly. "Look!"

He opened his beak. Nestling under his tongue was a small, brightly wrapped parcel.

"It's from the Lucky Dip!" cried Ben, taking the little package and tearing it open. "Awesome!"

He unwrapped a small remote-controlled car.

"Double awesome!" declared Max.

Jelly saluted and scuttled off.

When the fête finished a few minutes later, Max and Ben had sold everything on their table.

"Just one job still left to do, Agent Black," said Ben. "We've got a delivery to make."

"Yup. One elephant delivery coming

up, Agent Neal," Max agreed.

They grabbed the box from under the table and set off for the churchyard.

The gargoylz were in the far corner, hidden from view by a yew tree and several large gravestones.

Azzan was breathing fire at some thistles laid out on a stone, and hymnbooks were scattered all over the grass.

"What's going on?" asked Max.

"Greetingz!" said Toby. "We're having our own fête."

"Azzan's doing a barbecue," explained Barney, "and the rest of us are Book Wanging!"

"The winner is the one who can hit the

stone angel on the nose," Zack told them. He picked up one of the hymnbooks and threw it excitedly in the air. It whizzed straight up, bounced off the church gutter and landed on Azzan, who staggered around dizzily and fell into a patch of dandelions.

"It was a jolly good fête," said Jelly.

"Spluttering gutterz!" chortled Toby. "I haven't had so much fun since Zack fiddled with the vicar's computer so that every word he typed came out as 'monkey'."

The spikes on Barney's back drooped a little. "It has been a good fête," he sighed, "but it would have been even better if there'd been some white elephants." He held up the knitted trunk-warmer sadly. "I kept this just in case."

Max and Ben couldn't stop huge smiles spreading over their faces.

"Well, it just so happens that there *was*

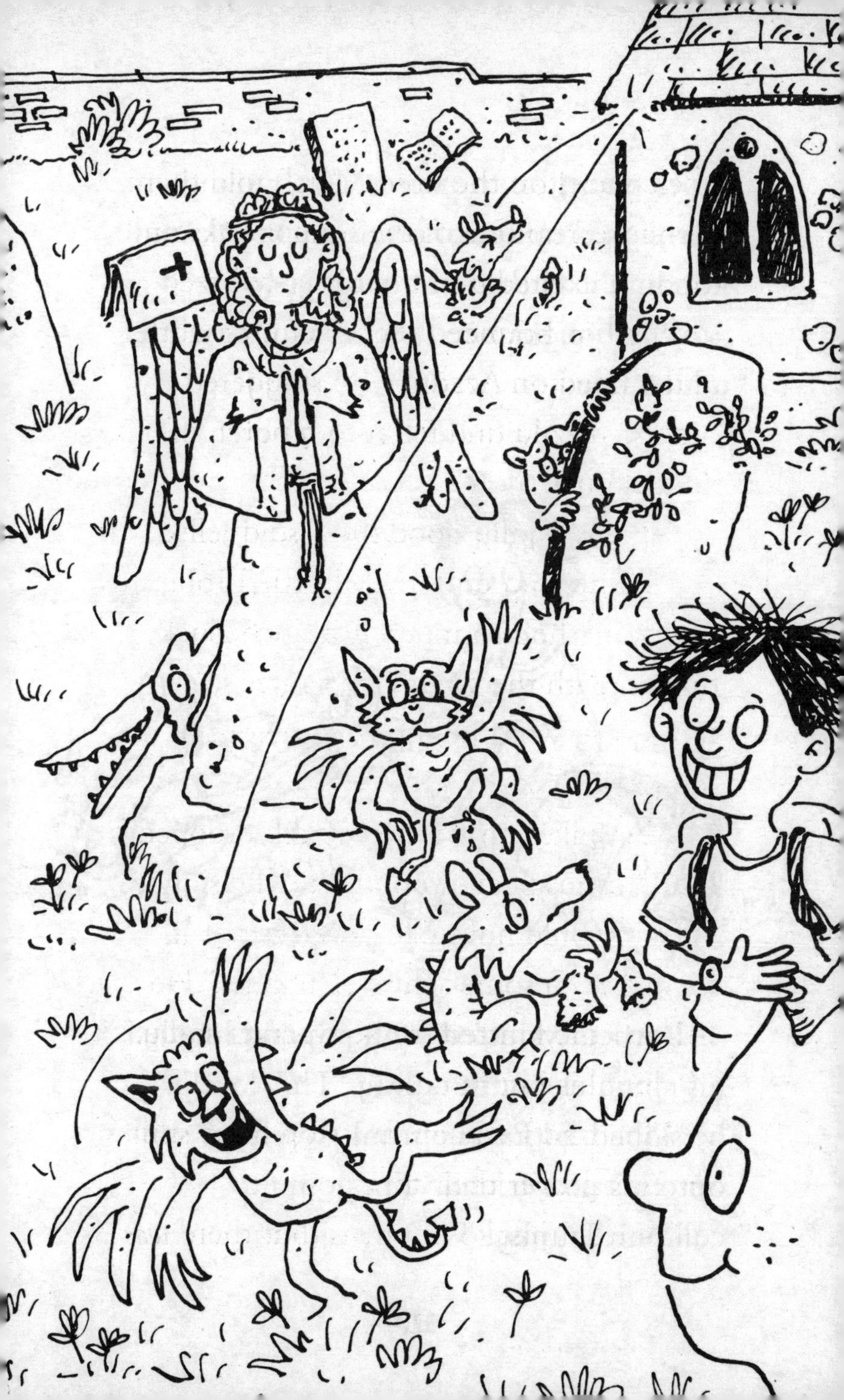

an elephant!" exclaimed Max, pulling
Barney's present out of his backpack and
handing it to the little gargoyle.

"We bought him specially for you,"
added Ben.

Barney wriggled with joy and hugged
his china elephant tightly. "He's lovely,"
he sighed, fitting the trunk-warmer
onto his new friend. "I'm going to
call him Trunky!"

"And he can sleep on the roof with us," added Toby.

"But no catapults!" Barney told Bart firmly.

"I love a happy ending," said Max with a huge grin.

"And this is the best happy ending in the history of best happy endings," agreed Ben.

Gargoylz Fact File

Full name: Tobias the Third
Known as: Toby
Special Power: Flying
Likes: All kinds of pranks and mischief – especially playing jokes on the vicar
Dislikes: Mrs Hogsbottom, garden gnomes

Full name: Barnabas
Known as: Barney
Special Power: Making big stinks!
Likes: Cookiez
Dislikes: Being surprised by humanz

Full name: Eli
Special Power: Turning into a grass snake
Likes: Sssports Day, Ssslithering
Dislikes: Ssscary ssstories

Full name: Theophilus
Known as: Theo
Special Power: Turning into a ferocious tiger (well, tabby kitten!)
Likes: Sunny spots and cosy places
Dislikes: Rain

Full name: Bartholomew
Known as: Bart
Special Power: Burping spiders
Likes: Being grumpy
Dislikes: Being told to cheer up

Full name: Nebuchadnezzar
Known as: Neb
Special Power: Changing colour
to match his background
Likes: Snorkelling
Dislikes: Anyone treading on his tail

Full name: Zackary
Known as: Zack
Special Power: Making himself
invisible to humanz
Likes: Bouncing around, eating bramblz,
thistlz, and anything with Pricklz!
Dislikes: Keeping still

Name: Azzan
Special Power: Breathing fire
Likes: Surprises
Dislikes: Smoke going up his
nose and making him sneeze

Full name: Jehieli
Known as: Jelly
Special Power: Turning to jelly
Likes: Having friendz to play with
Dislikes: Bulliez and spoilsports

Name: Ira
Special Power: Making it rain
Likes: Making humanz walk the plank
Dislikes: Being bored

Name: Cyrus
Special Power: Singing lullabies to send humanz to sleep
Likes: Fun dayz out
Dislikes: Snoring

Name: Rufus
Special Power: Turning into a skeleton
Likes: Playing spooky tricks
Dislikes: Squeezing into small spaces